Julia Jones' Diary

Book 2

My Secret Bully

Katrina Kahler

Table of Contents

Fear...

"PLEASE HELP MEEEEEEE!"

I could hear a piercing scream but the scene was so surreal that I felt almost sure the sound was coming from someone else and not me. The terror I felt in that moment was like nothing I'd ever experienced before and seemed to engulf me in a fear so suffocating that I found it difficult to breathe.

"How can this be happening?" I thought. "How can Sara have done this to me?" The vision of her face flashed quickly through my mind and even then, I could feel the evil that seemed to pour from every part of her.

Blood oozed from a deep gash on my hand and my pulse was racing so wildly I thought my heart would explode. "What if I bleed to death?" was all I could think as I banged harder on the tightly closed shed door. "LET ME OUT!" I screamed for what seemed like the millionth time and my voice grew croaky and hoarse. So much so that I was convinced this was the end. No one was coming to save me.

With a last ditch attempt, I shoved once more on the wooden door and to my utter surprise, it abruptly flew open. As I regained my balance, I stood still for a moment, in shock that I had managed to escape. And then I started to run.

Blindly, I raced through the dense bush land and felt so grateful at least, for the moon that shone down giving me the light I needed to find my way. Not that I had a clue in which direction I should be heading, but I knew I had to keep moving. The cut on my hand was bad and the faster I ran, the faster the blood seemed to flow.

I'd felt so claustrophobic back in that shed. As soon as I'd realized I had been locked in and that no one would be nearby to hear my screams for help, I just had to get out by any means possible. Even though I knew in my heart, there would be no way I'd fit through the tiny window, I had to try anyway. But removing the thick glass louvers was a big mistake and the broken pane sliced deeply into my skin. By the sliver of moonlight that shone through the remaining glass, I had seen that the gash was serious. Then within seconds, my hand was covered in pools of blood. The realization that more than ever, I desperately needed to escape, gave me the adrenalin I needed to break the door open.

As I scanned the forest surrounding me, trying to decide which direction to take, I wondered if I would actually make it back to the campsite. Then staggering, I took another step forward and collapsed heavily onto the ground.

My last thoughts as I slipped into unconsciousness were of Sara and how this whole disastrous problem had begun so many months ago. I'd been so happy back then and thoughts of the nightmare that was ahead were nonexistent in my mind.

Five months earlier...

I did not want to go to school! I absolutely dreaded the thought of walking into that classroom and facing her again. As I rolled over in bed, I hoped that Mom just might let me have the day off but it was not to be. "Hurry up, Julia! You need to get out of bed right now, or you're going to miss the bus!" Mom was calling to me from downstairs and I could tell by her tone that if I didn't show my face at the breakfast table within the next 60 seconds, I'd be in serious trouble.

"Why the sad face?" she asked me as I sat down to my bowl of cereal with a huge sigh. "I'm just tired," was all I replied. "Early to bed tonight," she said. "You've been having way too many late nights!"

"Yeah, whatever," I mumbled under my breath, so that she couldn't hear me. She really didn't have a clue what was going on at school. She thought that everything was just fine! Mrs. Jackson had given her rave reviews about my behavior and progress at the parent – teacher interview last month, so Mom just assumed that I was having another great year.

But the truth of the matter is that I hate going to school. It's the last place I want to be each day and the thought of going, just makes me feel sick.

It never used to be like this. I used to love school. I've always been an A student and there's never really been any problems before. But this year is different – totally different and school is the last place I want to be!

It all changed a few months ago, when Sara Hamilton came to our school. All the girls were really excited to have someone new join our class and Mrs. Jackson asked me to look after Sara and show her around. "That's fine," I had said. I was more than happy to be given this job – I actually felt honored to be chosen. But looking back now, I totally regret that day and my willingness to be Sara's friend.

At first, she was very nice – really friendly and outgoing and I could see all the girls were desperate to spend time with her. She wore the coolest clothes and was so pretty. The other girls soon started arguing about who was going to sit next to her during lunch breaks.

Of course she was happy to be getting so much attention. I mean who wouldn't be? Starting at a new school can be a kid's worst nightmare, but not for Sara. Everything seemed to work out for her and within a matter of days, she was constantly surrounded by the other girls in the class, including all my friends. And then all of a sudden, no one even knew that I existed any more.

I can cope with Sara being popular. I think she'd be popular wherever she went. She's so pretty and chatty and everyone thinks she's really cool – including the boys. But for some reason, she hates me! And she has made sure everyone else knows it.

The minute I walk into the room now, I see the girls whispering and then start giggling. It's so obvious that they're talking about me. "Where did you get your shoes, Julia?" Sara asked me the other day. "Did they have a sale on at the cheap shop?"

I couldn't help turning bright red, and the snickering I heard coming from the other girls only added to my embarrassment. These girls used to be my best friends. I can't believe that they can be so mean! Just because they think Sara is cool and they want her to like them. How can they be so horrible?

If only she had never come to our school and especially not my class, this would never have happened!

A disappearing act...

"Hurry up and sit down," Mrs. Jackson called out to our class as we noisily entered the room after lunch one Monday afternoon. "I have something important to tell you all!" For your technology project this term, you're going to design and construct a lunar lander. This is part of our unit of work on Space exploration and you'll be testing your constructions by launching them off the railing of the classroom veranda onto the concrete 30 feet below us.

"Awesome!" pretty much everyone in the class was calling out and getting really excited about the thought of this project. This was going to be something fun for a change. And it got even better because Mrs. Jackson told us that our astronauts would consist of a raw egg in a shell that we could decorate and protect in any way we wanted. But the main aim was to ensure a safe landing so that they actually survived and didn't end up splattered all over the concrete.

Everyone was excited and I could hear people coming up with ideas already. Alexander, who's the class genius especially when it comes to science, started listing all the detailed and technical stuff that he was going to attach. This included a jet propelled engine and a heap of scientific terminology that I'd never even heard of before.

Now technology isn't my best subject by any means but this sounded like a fun project and I am pretty creative. So I was hoping I could come up with something really good and get an A. In our science test last week, I scored a B+ which Sara scoffed at when she saw my mark.

"Only a B?" she asked me, with that mocking tone of hers.

"It's a B+, actually!" I thought to myself, but I kept my

mouth shut before saying something I knew I'd regret.

"Never mind," she said to me, "we can't all get A's!" and walked off with a huge smirk.

After that incident I felt more determined than ever to get a better mark for my project than she did and when I went home that night, I searched on the internet for as many ideas as I could possibly find.

That weekend, I looked around the house and in the garage for materials that would be suitable for my project. Mrs. Jackson had told us to bring everything to school on Monday so we could get started as soon as possible. In the end, I had so many bits and pieces that Mom had to drive me to school because I couldn't carry it all.

I'd designed and tested a really effective parachute on the weekend by dropping it off the family room balcony, complete with a raw egg in a basket. I was so happy to see that my little astronaut had survived – even though it did have a soft landing as the wind had blown it into our swimming pool and I then had to race to the rescue before it got sucked into the filter system. However, my parachute had obviously worked and I planned to make a much better and more detailed design at school.

Unfortunately though, during morning recess I started to feel quite ill and when Mrs. Jackson saw how deathly white my face was, she decided to call my mom to come and get me and take me home.

After a visit to the doctor, I spent the next 24 hours in bed. He said I had a flu bug that was going around and bed rest was what I needed. I didn't mind too much because it meant that I wouldn't have to go to school and face Sara, for a day at least.

I was glad to go back on Wednesday though, as that was the day we were going to begin our project and I had so many great ideas for mine. I couldn't wait to get started.

But then, as everyone was sorting through all the materials that they'd brought to school, I was left searching for the overstuffed bag that I'd brought in on Monday. It had been full to the brim and I was sure that I'd left it in the corner at the back of the room but it was nowhere to be seen.

Mrs. Jackson helped me to search but neither of us could find it anywhere! My heart began to sink as I watched all the other kids engrossed in their designs which were quickly coming together. Then all of a sudden, one of the boys called out, "Is this Julia's bag?"

He was holding up a large green bag that certainly looked like mine except that it was empty. "I found it stuck behind the cupboard at the back," he said. "A corner of it was poking out and that's how I spotted it."

The look of horror on my face when I saw that empty bag must have been completely obvious because Mrs. Jackson asked, "Does anyone know what has happened to all the materials that Julia brought in on Monday?"

I instantly looked towards Sara and our eyes met. She had this kind of half grin attached to her face as she answered, "No, Mrs. Jackson, I have no idea!"

I just couldn't believe it! I was completely convinced that Sara was somehow to blame but I had no proof. How could someone stoop so low? And what was I going to do? I had no materials whatsoever and the project had to be finished by the end of the week. This was a disaster!

Then to my huge surprise, Blake Jansen, the cutest boy in our class and the boy I've had a crush on since the fourth grade, suddenly offered to share his materials with me. I always knew that he was nice. He's nice to everyone and that's why he's so popular. And he's so good looking!

He was in my dance troupe for the school musical earlier in the year but that musical ended in my worst day ever, a day so bad that I will never forget it! Since then, Sara has taken up all his time and attention and I didn't think he even knew I existed anymore.

So I could not believe that he was actually offering to share with me. One minute I was absolutely devastated and the next I felt I was the luckiest girl on the planet. I shyly accepted and sat down next to him to start work. When I looked in Sara's direction though, the look of disgust in her eyes was like a red hot poker burning right through me and

I knew instantly that she was not happy. This had definitely not worked out the way she had planned.

I smiled briefly in her direction and then turned my back towards her while continuing to work on my project, alongside Blake. He had brought a heap of really cool stuff to school and there were lots of bits that he didn't need, which was very lucky for me. I also knew that I could probably find more things at home that night and bring them the next day, which is what I did. When I gave Blake some really thick foam padding so he could also add it to his construction, he looked at me, smiled and said, "Thanks Julia!" In that moment my heart skipped a beat and I thought to myself, "Maybe school isn't so bad after all!"

Sabotage...

Friday afternoon finally came and the whole class was so excited. We were going to test our lunar landers and everyone was lined up along the balcony ready for the launch. Mrs. Jackson had handed us a raw egg each which we'd been allowed to decorate and then place in the capsules that we'd constructed. Already there had been a few accidents with astronauts not even surviving the preparation stage and the remains of broken egg shell and gooey egg were scattered across the classroom floor. Luckily though, Mrs. Jackson had some spare eggs that she was able to hand out.

One at a time, we tested our designs. Most of the landings were actually successful, although there were a few astronauts that didn't survive and met their death on the concrete 30 feet below us. I was the last person to launch mine and everyone waited with anticipation as they'd all agreed that my design was actually the best. I'd spent so much time working on it and had come up with some really creative ideas. I did feel really proud and it was nice to be the one getting some attention for a change. Although it was clearly obvious from the way that Sara was staring at me that she was not impressed.

During the testing of the landers, I'd been sent to the administration office to collect some notes that were due to go home that afternoon. But I'd quickly rushed back so that I could finally test my creation. When I carefully picked it up, it seemed that the parachute strings had become tangled somehow and it actually felt heavier than what I'd originally thought.

Mrs. Jackson was telling me to hurry up as it was almost

home time and I needed to be quick. So I had no time to check what was causing the problem. With eager anticipation, I released my lander over the balcony railing edge but to my sheer horror, it literally dive bombed to the ground.

"Aa Haah!" I heard someone laugh almost hysterically. "It's committed suicide!" And the whole class cracked up with amusement at the sight of yellow egg yolk splattered all over the concrete below.

"So much for your creative design, Julia Jones!" sniggered Sara as she walked past with that familiar smirk which I'd come to know so well. And off she ran with her entourage of friends, all laughing at me and shouting, "Did you see Julia's? What a crack up!"

And I was left trying to clean up the mess off the concrete while everyone else headed home for the weekend.

As I inspected my lander, I was shocked to see that some small weights from the classroom math kit had been placed into the basket area and hidden under the egg. This was what had created so much weight in my design and caused the dive bomb that we had all witnessed. Along with that, the strings were all tangled which made the parachute completely ineffective, regardless of the extra weight.

I knew straight away, that this was Sara's handiwork. But what could I do? There was no way that she'd own up to it and who would believe me anyway? So much for hoping for a good mark - I'd be lucky to get a C for this project.

On the bus ride home, I miserably wondered if there was any way I'd be allowed to change schools. I didn't want to go back there on Monday or ever again.

Dancing mishap...

With sheer dread, I forced myself to go to school the following week but the sick feeling in the pit of my stomach would not go away. Every chance she got, I saw Sara watching me and as soon as she had my attention, she would whisper to one of the other girls. Then they'd both start giggling at some joke that she had made, all the while staring in my direction just to make sure I was aware they were talking about me.

I was miserable! I spent every lunch break in the library, too scared to go out to the playground for fear of facing Sara. I felt sure that she was making it her life mission to focus on me and humiliate me as often as possible.

When Friday came I was so relieved as the weekend ahead gave me two days where I wouldn't have to face her. Fridays are my favorite school day anyway because in the afternoons, we have dance class which is the lesson that I look forward to most.

Dancing is something I really enjoy and I'm pretty good at it. Every few weeks we work on a different style and this particular week, it was going to be hip hop. I couldn't wait because this is the style that I like best.

I go to hip hop classes every Saturday morning and our dance troupe is now practicing for a major competition that's coming up. If we make the top 3, we may be given the chance to compete at nationals, which will be amazing!

After working through some new moves with us, our dance teacher, Miss Brown chose me to go onto the stage and demonstrate some moves of my own to the other kids so that we could add these to the routine we were practicing. I was more than happy to do this as I'm quite confident with choreography and love being creative with new dance moves. But to my horror, she also chose Sara to go up onto the stage as well.

I knew that Sara was also a very good dancer. After the musical, everyone had nominated her as the best dancer in the school, so I really wasn't surprised that she had been chosen. The chances of us being up there together though were beyond belief. Especially as I had vowed that I would never dance with her again!

The whole of the seventh grade is involved in these classes each Friday afternoon and every pair of eyes was on Sara and I. One at a time, we were asked to demonstrate something that could possibly be added to the routine we were putting together while the rest of the grade looked on. I actually thought that finally I had a chance to outshine Sara and perform better than her. I was desperately hoping that Miss Brown would choose my moves as being the best.

Then, just as I took some lunging steps forward, I felt myself go flying through the air. It seemed as though everything was in slow motion and I was gliding through space. I could not work out what was happening until I abruptly and noisily face planted onto the stage floor, sliding to a stop right at Miss Brown's feet.

The hysterical laughter coming from probably every single grade 7 kid who was there that day just added to my humiliation and as I quickly stood up, the look of triumph in Sara's eyes was something I will never forget.

Once again, I knew that she was at fault and had taken the perfect opportunity to totally embarrass me in front of not only my own class but the entire grade.

Later on, Millie, the one and only true friend that I had left, confirmed my suspicions.

"Sara stuck her foot out and tripped you, Julia! I was sitting right in front of her and saw it. I can't believe she did that!"

I looked at Millie in dismay and then burst into tears.

"You have to tell Mrs. Jackson, Julia. You just have to!" We'd had this conversation numerous times before. But the truth of the matter was that I felt scared to tell a teacher for fear of what Sara would do if she found out. Plus, I didn't think it would solve the problem anyway.

There was a boy in our class last year named Billy, who was badly bullied and it got so intense that he ended up leaving our school. When the teacher had tried to intervene and help solve the problem, the bullying kept happening regardless. And one afternoon, Billy was even bashed up on his way home from school.

"That's your punishment for dobbing on us," is apparently what he was told by the group of boys who had ganged up on him. "Do it again and you'll get much worse next time. You'll see!"

Billy never came back to school after that and we heard that he now goes to another school. I just hope that it's worked out for him and that he has some nice kids in his class. He certainly didn't deserve to be bullied the way he was.

I've thought about telling my mom about the dramas with Sara but when I've told her about friendship problems that have happened before, she simply told me to find someone nicer to spend my time with. She just doesn't understand, so I'd rather keep it to myself.

I haven't even told Millie how bad it has become. In my head though, it's all I can think about and rather than focusing on homework these days, I've been trying to come up with ways to get Sara back. She is constantly in my thoughts and I think of very little else.

Yesterday, I started crying for no reason whatsoever. Mom was in the middle of talking to me and I burst into tears. "What's wrong with you, Julia?" was all she could say. "For goodness sake, why are you so emotional at the moment?"

But I couldn't bring myself to answer. I just turned my back, ran upstairs to my room and threw myself onto my bed. I had no one to talk to who would understand or who could help me. I had absolutely no one to turn to. I didn't know what to do!

Desperate...

At school the next week, Sara was bragging about these new high heel shoes that her mom had bought for her and she even brought them to school one day so she could show them off to everyone. They were really cool beige platforms with big silver buckles around the ankles.

There was no way my mom would ever let me wear anything like that. "You've got plenty of time for grown up clothes," is what she said to me when I'd asked for a pair of high heels myself.

"They will make you look so much older and you're only twelve. That's way too young!"

And that was the end of that. I'd only just convinced her to let me have a pair of skinny jeans. She didn't even want me wearing them as she thought they weren't appropriate for young girls. Did she expect me to look like a little girl my entire life?

It was hard to comprehend that she really was young herself once. I wished I had a fashionable mom who let me wear cool clothes and jewelry. Sara was always in the latest gear. She had so many cool clothes, it made me sick! And endless pairs of really nice shoes as well.

One night that week I dreamed that we were at the school fair. Sara had been chosen to represent the eleven to twelve year old age group in a fashion show. She had to walk along a cat walk modeling some new cool designs for tweens and all the girls at school were so envious.

She wore her beige platforms with the silver buckles and I was secretly hoping that she'd trip and make a fool of herself. But instead, something even better happened. When she put on the clothes that she'd been given to wear in the show, for some reason they were extremely tight on her and as she walked to the front of the cat walk stage, the zip burst entirely open and buttons started popping off into the audience. All she could do was try to hold the outfit together by pulling it across her body and run off the stage as quickly as possible. Everyone in the audience gasped with horror at the sight of a young girl racing in embarrassment off the catwalk while her clothes seemed to fall apart right there in front of them.

It was the best dream I've ever had! If only it could come true!

But unfortunately, I really couldn't see that happening. Knowing my luck, in real life Sara would blitz the show and become even more popular.

As I sat there recalling my dream, my mother's voice broke through my thoughts. "Julia, hurry up and eat your breakfast. You're going to be late for school!"

"Leave me alone! " I yelled, and raced out the front door slamming it shut.

I threw my school bag angrily over my shoulder and raced down the street.

Going to school that day was the furthest thing from my mind and before I knew it, I had walked past the bus stop and was headed into town. Skipping school was something I had never done before, but at that moment, I didn't care. I wanted to be as far away from school and Sara as possible.

I started wondering what I was going to do all day. I couldn't go home because Mom wouldn't have left for work yet, so I had to kill time somehow. Then the downtown shopping mall appeared ahead and I figured, why not? Browsing around the shops was as good a choice as any. Even though I was in my school uniform, I really didn't care! Things couldn't get any worse than they already were and I needed something to cheer me up.

My favorite clothes shop was the perfect place to start and within seconds, a pretty blue skirt caught my eye. It was in the latest style and I knew that it would be perfect to wear to the school disco on Friday night. I quickly flicked through the rack and found my size, thinking that I might ask to try it on.

As I glanced around looking for a sales assistant and realized that no one was in sight, a spontaneous and unexpected thought entered my mind. Without hesitation, I grabbed the skirt, shoved it into my school bag and raced out the door. The thudding of my heart sounded deafening in my ears and I felt certain that others must hear it as well and I would surely be caught.

"Hey you!" the gruff male voice nearby sent shivers of fear down my spine and I waited for the sound of heavy footsteps in hot pursuit behind me.

The burst of adrenalin that overtook me in that moment was like nothing I'd ever felt before and I soon found myself breathless at the corner of my street, my house and safety only a few minutes away.

As I raced through the front door and bolted it locked, I prayed that I was fast enough to have escaped and promised myself never to try anything as stupid ever again.

"What are you doing home, Julia?" my mother's voice called from the hallway. The bolt of shock at the sound of her voice made my knees buckle and I almost collapsed on the spot. "Are you alright? You don't look well!"

As I leaned against the wall shivering with guilt, convinced that I'd been found out, she abruptly ushered me upstairs and into my room. "You need to get to bed. Thank goodness you've come home, Julia. You're obviously not well enough for school today."

The relief I felt right then, as I climbed into bed was so intense, that I soon drifted off into a restless sleep but not before a vision of Sara's mocking eyes and a deep premonition of evil passed through me.

Blake...

Facing school the following day was more difficult than I could ever have imagined but to my utter amazement, the morning passed by without incident. Sara seemed completely absorbed in organizing details for the school disco that had been arranged for Friday night. Every time I dared to steal a glance in her direction, she and the other girls appeared to be engrossed in excited conversation and for the moment, I was apparently the furthest thing from Sara's mind.

I took advantage of the respite and even managed to relax a little. Then, just as I was about to enter the classroom after lunch, I felt a gentle tap on my shoulder.

"Hi Julia, I was just wondering if you're going to the disco on Friday night?"

"Aah, aah, I'm not sure," I stammered.

The sight of Blake Jansen, his dreamy brown eyes looking down into mine as he waited for my reply, caught me by total surprise and I could feel my face turning bright red. This was something that I could not avoid and I was often teased by my friends about how obvious it was when I was embarrassed. I was unable to stop the red glow and I stood there desperately hoping that the burning sensation I could feel would go unnoticed.

Without hesitation, he continued rather shyly, "It's just that I'm planning on going and I thought it might be fun if we could hang out there together." He must have misread the look of shock on my face as his expression quickly turned to apprehension, "Oh, only if you want to. But if you don't, then that's ok."

Just as he was about to turn and walk away, I forced myself to speak up. "Oh, that would be fun Blake. I'd love to hang out with you there."

"Awesome!" was his reply and the glowing smile that quickly appeared made my heart melt.

I could not believe it! Blake Jansen wanted to hang out with me at the disco! Was this a date? Was he actually asking me on a date? Did this mean that we were going out?

"Don't get carried away, Julia Jones!" I said to myself. "He just wants to hang out with you, that's all. He's just being nice."

But I could not wipe the grin from my face and as I sat down next to Millie, she asked. "What are you so happy about, all of a sudden?"

"Oh, nothing," was my reply. And we settled down for the afternoon lesson.

Not that I was able to concentrate after that. All I could think about was what I would wear on Friday night and how much fun it was going to be, especially being Blake Jansen's date! 'Perhaps I'll wear my new blue skirt after all,' I thought. 'I may as well not let it go to waste!' And as I sat on the bus heading home that afternoon, picturing in my mind Blake and I together at the disco, for the first time in weeks I did not give Sara even a single fleeting thought.

The disco…

Finally Friday night arrived. The disco was all anyone at school could talk about and I started to think that Sara had finally forgotten about me. She had much more interesting things to focus on now and I began to believe that my luck was beginning to change, definitely for the better.

As I peered at the reflection staring back at me from my bedroom mirror, I was suddenly overcome with guilt. "Should I wear this blue skirt, or not?" The same thought kept going around and around in my head. I had never stolen anything before and deep down I knew that it was wrong.

Acting on impulse the way I had was so unlike me and the feelings of remorse that I was now experiencing were totally overwhelming. I quickly pulled the skirt off, glad that it still had the tags attached and rummaged through my cupboard looking for something else to wear. A purple and green dress that Millie had given me just the week before, grabbed my attention and I gratefully put it on.

"I have to take that blue skirt back," I thought adamantly. "I'm going to go back to the shop next week and own up to what I did." I felt sick with anxiety at the thought of facing the shop assistant with my story, but I knew that it had to be done.

Hearing the honk of a car horn outside, I pushed all thoughts of the stolen skirt from my mind and raced down the stairs. Where did you get that dress from, Julia?" Mom asked as I headed out the front door. "I've never seen you wear that before and isn't it a little short?"

A confrontation with Mom was the last thing I wanted, so I

quickly replied, "Millie gave it to me because it doesn't fit her properly. Anyway, I've gotta go. I think her dad has just pulled up in our driveway. I don't want to keep them waiting. Bye!" And with that, I was gone.

I felt a pang of guilt thinking once more of the stolen skirt hidden in the back of my cupboard. Mom would be so disappointed if she knew I had actually stolen something. Taking a deep breath, I promised myself that I would definitely return it the following week.

Once inside the disco, I became dizzy with excitement and when I spotted Blake across the dance floor, the butterflies in my stomach went absolutely crazy.

"This is so cool!" Millie exclaimed. "Who would ever think that our school hall could look so amazing?"

The hall had been decorated with flashing lights and there was a mirror ball hanging right in the center. The effect of the little white lights spinning across the walls and floor really was cool and it was hard to believe that it actually was our school hall.

I waved to Blake and he began to head across the floor in my direction. The music was really loud and already kids were dancing. "Come on! Let's dance!" yelled Millie, grabbing my arm and dragging me onto the dance floor.

I looked back towards Blake but he had disappeared amongst the crowd that had gathered at the sound of one of the latest hit songs being played.

Everyone was singing the words and the noise was deafening. I could actually feel vibrations through the floor.

Millie and I had to yell to each other to be heard. "This is so much fun!" she screamed. "Let's keep dancing!"

I reluctantly stayed for another song, all the while, scanning the hall for Blake, but couldn't see him anywhere.

Then, without warning, I was roughly shoved in the back and went flying forwards falling onto a girl who was dancing with a group of friends beside me. "Sorry!" I mouthed helplessly, trying to be heard over the raging drum beat.

As I turned to see what had caused me to overbalance, my face fell. "Oops! I'm SO sorry Julia!" Sara's blazing eyes, stared vindictively into mine as she pushed past me pulling on Blake's hand and dragging him into the center of the dance floor.

I looked on in total dismay as she turned back with a smirk then disappeared with Blake amongst the crowd of kids dancing to the loud music.

"I don't feel well," I shouted into Millie's ear and then quickly darted off to the bathroom.

I hadn't told her about Blake and how I felt about him. I just wanted to keep it to myself and at that point I was glad that I had. Once again I felt humiliated and stupid. How could I think that he would really be interested in a girl like me? The cutest boy in our grade and I honestly believed that he might like me.

"How dumb am I!" was all I could think to myself. Sara probably set the whole thing up and once again she succeeded in making me look like a fool.

Millie had come after me, to check that I was ok. I felt bad as I didn't want to spoil her fun. We'd both been so looking forward to the disco and it wasn't fair of me to ruin it for her. "I'm ok. You go and enjoy yourself. I'll come out and join you soon."

I managed to convince her that I wouldn't be long and eventually she agreed. But all the while, I just wanted to go home. I craved the sanctuary of my bedroom where I could just hide away and not see anybody. I was so grateful that I didn't have to go to school the following day. That would have been unbearable.

Finally it was time to leave and Millie's dad arrived to take us home. I pretended I was busy over the weekend when Millie asked what I had planned. I just didn't feel like seeing or talking to anybody.

When Mom asked if I'd had a good time, I quickly replied, "Yes, it was great but I'm really tired. I'm going to bed."

As I rushed upstairs to my room and fell onto the covers, I pressed my face into the pillow and within seconds it was wet with tears. I chokingly stifled my sobs for fear of being heard. I'd never felt so unhappy.

The Cyber Bully…

"WHAT?" I screamed when Millie told me the news on Monday morning. "Oh no! What am I going to do?" I was absolutely mortified. I just couldn't believe what I was hearing. When was this nightmare ever going to end?

"I couldn't believe it either!" cried Millie. "I quickly checked Facebook this morning before I left for school and there it was staring at me…Julia Jones desperately wants a boyfriend. Anyone interested?… And there were already 15 likes and 3 comments. But you don't want to know what they were!"

FB needs DISLIKE!!

Could things honestly get any worse? The idea that Sara would post something like that about me on Facebook was beyond comprehension.

"Why is she doing this?" Millie asked. "I mean, seriously! What is her problem?"

I felt ill. I wasn't allowed to have Facebook and would have had no idea about this latest turn of events. But some of the kids at school used Facebook regularly and word spread pretty quickly. Already I was getting strange looks from both girls and boys who obviously had already seen it for themselves or heard all about it.

"You have to tell Mrs. Jackson!" Millie demanded. "If you don't tell her, then I will!"

I knew in my heart that she was right. Someone had to be told. This had gone too far. But a voice inside my head was warning me. "Don't do it – it'll make things even worse!"

Then, before I had a chance to consider further the consequences of what I was about to do, Millie dragged me over to the teacher's desk where Mrs. Jackson was sitting.

"Mrs. Jackson," she said forcefully, "Julia has something to tell you!"

As we later waited outside the principal's office, the looks that Sara was giving me were nothing less than frightening. I didn't dare glance her way and the nauseating feeling in the pit of my stomach only contributed to the anxious thoughts rushing through my mind. I was filled completely with dread.

But why was I feeling this way? I had done nothing wrong. For some reason I felt guilt ridden, as if it were all my fault. How could I let her have so much power over me?

"Do you know that this sort of thing is considered cyber bullying, Sara?" Mrs. Harding, the principal asked when we had been seated in her office.

"Oh, Mrs. Harding, I'm so sorry," cried Sara innocently. "I didn't mean to upset Julia at all. She's been jealous of me since the day I came to this school and I simply felt sorry for her. I've been getting so much attention from all the girls and boys in our class and Julia just hasn't coped. So, I thought that I might be able to help her feel more popular. I just want her to know that I care about her and there's absolutely no reason to feel jealous of me! All I want to do is to be her friend."

I could not believe the words I was hearing, nor the convincing spiel that was coming from Sara's mouth. The sweet, little girl act that I was witnessing was deserving of an award, it was so good. And the big problem was that I could see she already had Mrs. Harding fooled.

"That's not true," I cried. "She's been horrible to me almost since the day she arrived. I've done nothing to her whatsoever but she's always doing and saying mean things to upset me. I HATE HER!"

"Julia! That's a terrible thing to say. Control yourself young lady!" Mrs. Harding's response was the last straw. What hope did I have?

"Sara, I'd like you to delete that post off Facebook and please take more care with how you use that site in future. I'm sure you didn't mean to offend Julia, but sometimes words can be misunderstood."

"Yes, of course, Mrs. Harding," Sara replied. "I'm so sorry to have caused any trouble and I'm so sorry Julia. All I want is for us to be friends!"

The look of total innocence on Sara's face made my skin crawl and I could barely stand to look at her. I was the first to leave that office. I couldn't get out of there quickly enough.

But Sara soon caught up with me. "You have no idea what I'm capable of! Dob on me again and you're dead!

The cruel twisted snarl of her mouth made her meaning perfectly clear and the spine tingling shiver I felt, as I headed back to class, filled me with fear.

 "What's going on, Julia?" Mom demanded as I walked in the front door later that afternoon. "This morning I got a phone call from your school principal and it certainly wasn't to tell me how wonderful you've been, that's for sure! Isn't

Sara Hamilton the new girl who started earlier this year? I thought you were good friends with her."

"Yeah, right!" I replied sarcastically. "That'll be the day!"

"Well with that attitude, no wonder there are problems! Now, you know that I do not agree with young girls having access to Facebook but according to Mrs. Harding, Sara was just trying to be nice to you!"

"And that's not all," she continued, frowning at the look of utter disgust that had obviously appeared on my face.

"Apparently there have been problems with your behavior in class as well. Mrs. Jackson has reported that you've been sullen and very distant, not wanting to join in at all with the other girls. And even your grades have dropped! Is something going on that I don't know about?"

"There's nothing going on," I replied. "Everything is fine!"

I was almost tempted to tell her… "Sara is a bully! I hate

her!! I never want to go back to school ever again!"

But I knew that it was no use. Mom would go straight to the principal's office and demand an explanation. Then I'd really be in trouble. The menacing and piercing look in Sara's eyes today, when she threatened me on our way back to class, was still fresh in my mind and there was no way I was going to tell anyone. And besides that, Mom just wouldn't understand.

I sighed and headed silently off up to my room. "Mrs. Harding is suggesting that you see the school counselor, Julia!" Mom's stern retort rang in my ears. "I think that I'm going to arrange an appointment. I don't know what's wrong with you these days. Your attitude is a disgrace!"

I quietly closed my bedroom door and sank down miserably onto the bed. My childhood teddy bear caught my eye and I reached over and drew him close. As I hugged him tightly, tears of despair fell silently onto his threadbare coat of brown matted fur. He'd been given to me for a first birthday present by some close family friends and from that day on we'd been inseparable. These days though, he was left to sit quietly alone on my cupboard shelf, almost forgotten.

"How can things have become so bad?" I asked him. And he stared silently back at me. I laid down clutching him tightly and soon fell into a deep and troubled sleep.

Do I want to go to camp?...

Everyone was abuzz at school the next day, eager with anticipation about the camp that was scheduled for the following week. We'd been asked to form ourselves into small groups and were going to be assigned a cabin each to sleep in. There was lots of excitement about the camp as it involved several very cool activities including horse riding, archery, whip cracking and a big campfire each night. These were things that most of us had never experienced before so it sounded like it was going to be awesome.

I had really been looking forward to it, but now I wasn't so sure. "What if Sara starts picking on me?" I thought. "Maybe I should make up some excuse and not go."

"But you HAVE to go to camp, Julia!" cried Millie when I told her that I was having second thoughts. "I'm not going without you and that's that! You can't miss out on camp. It's the highlight of the whole year. And besides, Sara will be too busy to be bothering with you. We'll just make sure that Mrs. Jackson puts us in different activity groups to Sara and then we'll have nothing to do with her!"

"Okay," I hesitatingly relented. "If we're in separate groups for everything and she's in a different cabin as well, it should be fine, I guess."

I also knew with absolute certainty that my parents would not let me drop out now, especially after everything had been confirmed and paid for.

But I soon discovered that it was a relief to take my mind off Sara. And as Millie and I organized ourselves into a group with some really nice girls from the other class, I too started to feel the excitement that had the whole grade buzzing.

While discussing camp arrangements with the others, an eerie feeling made me turn quickly around and I had a strange sensation that someone was watching me.

As I glanced towards the back of the room, I realized that

Blake Jansen was staring in my direction. "What's his problem?" I wondered. "Hasn't he humiliated me enough already? Go and find another girl whose feelings you can crush," I thought to myself and abruptly turned my back on him.

Later that day, we all went off to dance class where Miss Brown announced that she would be holding a dance competition during the last week of term.

The idea was for groups of dancers to compete against each other in a dance off and the rest of the school would vote to decide on the winning group. This was to be part of a fun activity day that was planned for the entire school and the prize for the winners was a $200 voucher for the group to spend at the local shopping center.

This was one of several prizes that had been donated to the Arts department and Miss Brown had decided that it would be a great way to promote dancing in the school, amongst both the girls and the boys. Each group could choose to perform whatever style of dance that they preferred and the idea was met with immediate approval from just about everyone.

Instantly, groups of kids started rushing towards each other, keen to form dance groups with their friends. Some of the boys in our grade are awesome at hip hop and I saw them gather quickly into a group, Blake Jansen included.

To my utter surprise, several girls also approached me, asking if they could please be in my group. I felt shocked as this was totally unexpected. I had thought for sure, everyone would want to be with Sara because she is so popular and obviously a very good dancer.

It felt really good to be involved in something that I love so much and actually be surrounded by girls who were keen to be with me. Maybe things were changing for the better! We arranged to get together at lunch time on Monday so we could begin to rehearse. I promised to spend the weekend choreographing some moves and everyone agreed that I should lead the group. For the first time in ages, I really had something to look forward to and I couldn't wait to get home so I could start putting a dance together.

As I turned to leave, Sara brushed roughly past me. "Don't get your hopes up, Julia! My group is obviously going to win. You don't have a hope!" And with a flick of her long hair, she strode haughtily out the door.

"Just ignore her," Millie whispered in my ear. "We're going to blitz this. You wait and see!"

"If only I had your confidence," I thought to myself. Then the familiar anxious feeling started to form in the pit of my stomach and quickly take over.

With my head down, I headed for the bus stop, deep in thought about the hip hop moves that I could incorporate into our dance. With so many girls counting on me, I knew I could not let them down.

But I didn't know if I was up to the task. Would we actually be able to outperform Sara and her group? I was not convinced that it was possible.

As I lay in bed later that night, the day's events rushed through my mind. First and foremost was the moment when I had returned the stolen blue skirt. The memory of walking into the clothing shop after school that day was one I will never forget. A look of recognition had crossed the face of the sales assistant as I strode hesitantly towards her, squeamish with anxiety and guilt. It had been such a daunting prospect and I had come really close to backing down. But the feeling of relief now that it was all over was very intense, and I knew that I would never attempt anything as stupid and dishonest again.

To my complete surprise though, the young woman had actually been very good about the whole incident. The look of shock that had first appeared on her face quickly disappeared when I explained that I had made a terrible mistake and was dreadfully sorry. She even thanked me for returning the skirt, saying that she was pleased I had the courage to do the right thing.

When I finally managed to close my eyes, thoughts of blue skirts and dance moves flashed through my mind and I tossed and turned for what seemed quite a long time before eventually falling asleep.

Things are getting worse...

Monday dawned bright and clear and I raced to school armed with my iPod and a range of dance moves that I had managed to choreograph over the weekend. I'd spent most of the time, in my room, searching You Tube for new ideas and practicing the moves that I had come across.

I was feeling fairly confident until I walked past the classroom window where I spied Sara and her group already rehearsing. They had obviously arrived at school very early and asked Mrs. Jackson for permission to use the classroom to practice.

What I saw stripped every bit of confidence I had previously been feeling, right from my mind. It was still early days but it was clear that what Sara had put together was extremely good.

"She is very creative!" I thought to myself. "I have to give her credit for that!" And then a smirk appeared on her sun tanned face as she turned towards the window and spotted me walking past.

"Can't you come up with moves of your own?" she snarled nastily at me. "Is your dance so hopeless that you have to come spying on us?"

I just put my head down and kept walking; desperately trying to hide the red blush that I knew was creeping up my cheeks and covering my entire face.

"Why do I let her get to me?" I moaned. Deep down I knew that was part of her power over me. She loved to make me squirm and the more I reacted, the more she attacked, thriving on every minute of my discomfort.

The words Mom called out to me as I raced out the door,

rushing to make the bus that morning, suddenly sprang to mind. "I really think that you should see that counselor, Julia. If you are having problems at school, then you should let someone know and if you won't talk to me, you might feel more comfortable speaking with her."

"I wonder if I should try talking to the counselor?" I asked myself.

Tracey Watson who is in my class, had a few sessions with her last year and she had said that it really helped. Apparently the counselor is very nice and she's fairly young as well. Maybe she would understand and give me some advice. I'd have to swear her to secrecy though. There's no way I want Sara finding out!

The thoughts that were racing through my head quickly disappeared when I bumped into Millie who was bouncing around with excitement at the thought of us all leaving for camp the following day.

"All the girls in our dance group are sharing our cabin as well," she reminded me. "So we may even get a chance at camp to have some rehearsals!"

"That would be really cool," I agreed. "The more practice we have the better because I can see that we're definitely going to need it!"

At lunch time, we ran through all the moves that I had choreographed and the girls were very impressed. We had decided on a hip hop dance as all of us love this style the best and it's what we're all good at. I started to feel my confidence return.

So far, our dance was coming along well and really was looking good. We promised each other that we'd practice at home and continue to meet up each lunch time the following week after returning from camp. I began to believe that we really might have a chance at winning, after all!

Camp...

There was a huge gathering of kids at school early the next morning all armed with sleeping bags, pillows and other essential gear that was required for the next 3 days at camp. As we lined up ready to board the bus, Millie must have sensed my apprehension. "Don't worry about Sara! It's all going to be fine and we're going to have a really great time," she exclaimed in a reassuring voice.

"You must be a mind reader!" I replied and managed a small smile.

As we climbed onto the bus, an uneasy feeling came over me and the involuntary shiver that passed down my spine made the hairs on my arms stand on end. I really hoped that Millie's words would ring true, but the little voice inside my head said otherwise.

After being briefed by the camp leaders, we were directed towards our cabins and told to unpack so we could get started on our first activity. Our group was scheduled to do archery and when we lined up to wait for our instructor, I saw Blake Jansen heading towards us with a group of other boys.

"What do they want?" I wondered crossly as I briefly made eye contact with Blake and then quickly looked the other way.

"Hey girls," called a boisterous kid named Jack Donaldson. "Guess what! We've been asked to join your group. Pretty cool, hey?"

"Great!" I replied sarcastically, as I rolled my eyes at him, "That's really made my day."

"I thought it might," he said smugly. "We can even show you a thing or two about archery. You girls probably don't have a clue how to use a bow and arrow."

That was all I needed, Jack Donaldson and Blake Jansen in our group for the entire camp. Seriously! What had I done to deserve this?

Once we got started though, I found that archery was actually really fun and it was so cool. I managed to hit a bull's eye.

"You're pretty good at this!" commented Blake as he stood back watching while I had my turn.

I ignored his comment and focused on the target, determined to prove that I could be just as good if not better than any of the boys and was secretly pleased when the arrow I shot hit the bull's eye once more.

"Nice shooting!" exclaimed the instructor. "You're a natural at this."

"Thanks!" I replied and couldn't keep the smile from my face especially when Jack's arrows never even managed to hit the target at all, not one of them.

I soon started to relax and enjoy myself. The weather was sunny and warm and our next activity was canoeing in the river, which we were all looking forward to. Perhaps Millie was right. This camp really was going to be awesome and I began to feel genuinely happy to be there.

At the river's edge, we were put into groups of four and assigned canoes. We all had to wear life jackets and listen to instructions as well as a safety talk before hopping in and paddling off.

Once we got going, we managed to set a pretty good rhythm

and before we knew it, our group had paddled quite a distance down the river.

"We'd better wait for the others," I said as we paddled around a sharp bend.

We had been told to stay within sight of the instructor so we decided to wait for them all to catch up. Within a minute or so, Blake and Jack's canoe appeared and then right behind them was the instructor.

Even though I was still annoyed with him, I couldn't help but think to myself, "How cool would it be if I was in Blake's canoe?" and I pictured the scene in my mind.

A couple of the other groups were struggling though and weaving all over the place; they just couldn't seem to get the hang of it.

Then without warning, I felt our canoe start to wobble. I

turned around to see what was causing it and to my horror, there was Cassie Jenkins, one of the girls in our group, standing and making her way to the front where I was sitting.

"What are you doing?" I called to her.

"Sit down," yelled Millie. "You'll make us capsize!"

And just as those words left Millie's lips, over we went. All four of us fell into the water. Now this wouldn't have been so bad but we could not turn the canoe over again and even though it was a warm day, the water was freezing!

As well as being cold, I felt totally embarrassed, especially with the boys watching. Our plan had been to prove that we could do everything better than them but now we were bobbing around in the freezing water feeling humiliated and embarrassed!

All the other groups were laughing hysterically and even the instructor thought it was funny watching us struggle to get our canoe flipped over again.

Just as I started to despair that we'd never manage it, a pair of hands appeared beside mine on the edge of the canoe and when I looked to see whose they were, Blake's head popped up from under the surface of the water. He had dived in to give us a hand and with his help we soon managed to get the canoe upright. As we clumsily clambered back in, we gave Cassie strict instructions to stay in one spot from then on.

"I just wanted to have a turn at the front," she wined. "I didn't mean to capsize the boat!"

"Well, thank goodness Blake helped us," said Millie. "Without him, we'd still be floating around in the freezing river!"

I glanced timidly in his direction but he was already paddling off.

"Yeah, that was a pretty nice thing for him to do," I commented. "No one else was in any hurry to help us."

While paddling back to our starting spot, I thought briefly about Blake and wondered why he was being so nice. I later put him out of my mind though, as our group headed down to the horse stables. Horse riding was going to be the highlight of the whole camp as only a few of us had ever ridden before.

"I'm nervous," said Cassie. "What if my horse takes off?"

"You'll be fine," replied Millie. "These horses are especially chosen for beginner riders. I've been on trail rides before and the horses are always very well-behaved."

"I hope so!" was Cassie's worried reply.

"Hi girls!" called a familiar voice from behind us. I turned quickly, absolutely appalled to see Sara Hamilton walking in our direction.

"What are you doing here?" asked Millie in an unfriendly tone.

"My group has too many in it, so I volunteered to join this one. I thought it would be really fun to go riding with you guys!"

Her smug retort made my stomach drop and a feeling of dread seemed to take control of my senses. She gave me a distinctly piercing look and then turned to smile sweetly at Blake.

"Hi Blake!" she exclaimed. "I didn't know you were in this group."

"Yeah, I bet you didn't." I thought to myself. And Millie and I exchanged sickened glances.

"Just ignore her," Millie whispered. "It'll be fine."

We were greeted by the riding instructors who helped to fit us each with a helmet and then asked if anyone had had experience with horses.

"Oh, Julia Jones knows how to ride!" exclaimed Sara loudly.

Once again, she had taken the opportunity to draw attention to me with the sole purpose of causing as much humiliation as possible and I was too overwhelmed to contradict her. Our dump in the river was enough embarrassment for one day, so I kept quiet.

"Well then Julia," the instructor said. "You can ride Jazzy. She's our most forward moving horse and is best for someone with experience."

The feeling of anxiety that I had become so acquainted with lately, overtook me. It was true that I had ridden before, but only a couple of times and I would hardly say that I was experienced. Now it was my turn to start feeling nervous.

We were all given instructions before mounting our horses and then asked to ride in a circle around the arena. After a few laps, we followed in a line out onto the trail with one of the instructors in the lead and one at the very rear.

Blake Jansen was furthest from my mind at that point, and I focused on the trail ahead.

I could feel that my horse, Jazzy wanted to get going and the slow pace that the instructor had set didn't seem to satisfy her. I pulled on the reins to slow her down but to no avail, she was keen to get moving.

"This is fun!" I heard Cassie call out from somewhere way behind me.

She'd been put on the slowest horse that was delegated to the rear and was obviously feeling quite safe. Sara was right in front of me on a beautiful white pony called Starlight. It was so typical that she had ended up with the prettiest horse of them all.

Then out of the blue and without warning Starlight kicked out with his back legs towards Jazzy, probably because Jazzy had been too close. Sara let out a piercing scream which completely startled Jazzy and then I screamed as well. Jazzy started to trot which quickly turned into a canter and before I knew what was happening, she had overtaken the instructor's horse and was bolting along the track.

My screams seemed to add to her excitement and before long she was at a full gallop. All I could do was hold onto the reins as tightly as I could in the hope of being able to stay on her. Tree branches brushed past me in a total blur and I soon closed my eyes as it was too terrifying to keep them open.

I have no idea how I managed to stay on that horse but after what seemed like an eternity, I could feel her start to slow down. I opened my eyes and realized that one of the instructors had caught up to me, grabbed Jazzy's reins and pulled her to a stop. I was in too much shock to say or do anything but when the instructor asked if I was ok, I burst into tears.

"It's ok," she said soothingly. "We're almost back at the stables. Jazzy got a fright and was heading home. I've never seen her behave like this before though, it is very unusual. I don't know what got into her today!"

She helped me to dismount and we both walked our horses back to the stables where the others were waiting. I could feel myself still shaking as everyone surrounded me, asking if I was ok. I noticed Blake looking on with concern. Sara stood back probably annoyed that I was getting so much attention.

By that stage, I'd had more than enough excitement for one day and strode past her ignoring her glaring look. All I wanted to do was go back to the cabin and be left alone for a while.

"Why did I agree to go on this camp?" I asked myself. "I should have known that it would be a disaster."

But nothing could have prepared me for what lay ahead.

The note...

After dinner that night and songs around the campfire, we all headed back to our cabins where we were told to get organized for bed. Totally exhausted from the day's events, I climbed onto one of the lower bunks where I had my sleeping bag neatly laid out. The other girls were still chatting excitedly, but I'd had quite enough by then and was desperately looking forward to some sleep.

When I opened the zip I spotted a piece of yellow paper stuck inside, partly hidden from view. Curious, I pulled it out and realized that a note had been roughly scribbled down and addressed to me...

Julia
Meet me at the horse stables at midnight.
Don't bring anyone!
Don't tell anyone!
Or you're DEAD!

I knew instantly who the note was from and looked

nervously around the cabin wondering if anyone had seen me reading it. But the girls were all too engrossed in trying to outdo each other with scary stories and hadn't even noticed what I was doing.

That familiar anxious feeling crawled up my spine and sent cold shivers throughout my entire body.

"What am I going to do?" I thought to myself. "What is Sara up to now?"

Fearfully, I climbed into bed and turned my head towards the wall, wondering why this was happening to me and knowing full well that if I went along there would be trouble.

But if I didn't go, it might get worse. Although, maybe she just wanted to settle our differences and become friends? I grasped hold of that thought, hoping desperately that it would be the case. Deep down inside however, I was sure that I would not be so lucky.

The meeting...

The sound of my alarm was muffled by the thick padding of my sleeping bag. I had hidden it under the covers so as not to disturb anyone but the alarm hadn't been necessary as there was no way that I could have fallen asleep. My stomach was in knots with anticipation over what lay ahead and I crept quickly and quietly out of bed, changed into some clothes and slipped silently out the door.

The beam of my flashlight shone brightly along the track. However, I didn't really need it as the light of the full moon was more than enough to guide me, and before I knew it, I had reached the stables.

I heard the nicker of a horse as I approached and when I peered inside, Sara's long blonde hair and cold blue eyes suddenly emerged from the darkness.

"I didn't think you'd come!" she said in a mocking tone.

"I didn't think I had a choice!" was my anxious reply. "What's going on Sara? What's this all about? Why can't you just leave me alone?" I questioned her, hoping for an answer at last.

"Come with me!" was her only response.

As we headed along the bush track, following the beam of her flashlight, I summoned the courage to ask, "Where are we going? Where are you taking me?"

I could feel myself shaking nervously but my curiosity was too much. I had to get to the bottom of this, once and for all.

"I have something to show you," she said. "Something you need to see!"

We walked silently on deeper and deeper into the bush and just as I was about to say, "This is enough! I'm going back!" we reached a small shed that was partly hidden amongst the trees.

"We're here!" she said, holding the door open wide. "Have a look inside and you'll see."

Although I felt overwhelmed with apprehension, I had become way too curious and took a step forwards into the darkened interior.

The sudden sound of the door slamming shut behind me followed by the click of a bolt filled me with dread. As I directed my flashlight back towards the door, I could see that it had been tightly closed and when I tried to push it open, it wouldn't budge.

Like a lightning bolt, the realization hit me. Sara had tricked me. She had locked me in and left. I banged fiercely on the door and screamed, "Sara, what are you doing? Let me out! Let me out! Please let me out!" But there was no reply.

Just before the beam of my flashlight dimmed to a tiny glow, I spotted one small window set into the corner of a wall and then I was left in darkness.

"Oh no, the batteries are dead!" I thought with total disbelief. "But this is crazy! How on earth could she have done this to me? She has to be insane!"

Then, panic stricken, I realized abruptly that my screams for help would not be heard and looked towards the window as my only means of escape.

It's all too much...

I sat up with a start. "Where am I? What am I doing here?"

These were the thoughts racing through my head as I groggily regained consciousness. "What happened to me?"

The throbbing pain in my hand caused me to look down and as I stared at the vivid pool of blood that had formed on the ground, my memory jolted back into focus.

The feeling of claustrophobia that had overcome me had been too much and I recalled my efforts to escape through the tiny window, even though I knew it would have been impossible to fit through.

The throbbing pain was a reminder of the glass louver that I had broken after trying to remove it from the window frame. And the rush of adrenalin I had felt after accidentally slicing my hand with broken glass was fresh in my mind. But that had given me the strength I needed to finally push the door open.

"I must have passed out just after I escaped," I thought to myself as I unsteadily got to my feet, looking around in the dim early morning light and feeling grateful at least that I could now see where I was going.

The sun was only just rising and with a quick glance around, I soon spotted a well-worn track to my left. I stumbled forwards, holding onto the gash on my hand, thankful that the blood had seemed to stop flowing.

I headed along the track, praying that it would lead me back to the campground and the safety of my cabin.

Before long, the stables appeared in full view and I felt weak with relief. I staggered up the hill towards my cabin and burst through the door only to find everyone still asleep in bed, completely oblivious to what I had been through.

"Millie!" I exclaimed as I shook her awake. "I think I need a doctor!"

The sequence of events from that moment on had become a total blur and all I could think about now was how grateful I was to be back at home and in the comfort and safety of my own bed. The look of concern on my mother's face as she hovered over me, sponging my forehead with a damp towel was the reassurance I needed and I sank into a deep and dreamless sleep.

"Julia Jones!" Mom exclaimed from the chair by my bedside where she had been sitting for the past several hours.

"I'm so glad you're awake. I've been worried sick about you!"

I looked down at my hand, realizing that it was covered in a thick white bandage.

"You have 10 stitches. And the doctor said that you lost a lot of blood. What on earth happened at camp, Julia? How did you end up like this?"

I looked into my mother's eyes and abruptly burst into tears.

"Why don't you start from the beginning?" her gentle, supportive tone was the prompt that I needed. And without another moment's hesitation, I poured forth the whole story, not skipping a single detail.

"Julia, you should have told me sooner!" she exclaimed. "I've had no idea what you've been going through all this time."

"I didn't think that you would understand," I burst out. "And I had no one that I could tell. I'm so scared Mom. I don't want to go back to school, ever!"

I lay there thinking about the nightmare that I had just been through, wondering if it had really happened. It all seemed too surreal.

"I'm going to make an appointment with your school principal tomorrow," Mom stated adamantly. "We need to get to the bottom of this. Sara obviously needs help. This situation has become out of control and dangerous. You should not have let it get this far!"

I felt helpless and scared. What if Mom made the situation worse! Why couldn't I just change schools anyway? Was this nightmare ever going to end?

Mom visits the school...

"I went to see Mrs. Harding today," said Mom as she walked into my room the following afternoon and sat down on my bed. "Apparently she was contacted by your teacher who informed her that you had to be taken to the hospital. Mrs. Jackson thinks that you must have tripped and fallen on some broken glass that was found outside your cabin."

"But that's not true!" I felt sick with dismay as the words my mother had spoken started to really sink in.

"Mrs. Harding reminded me of your attitude towards Sara since her arrival at the school and as well as that, your outburst when you were called to her office last week."

The look of skepticism on Mom's face showed that she was now having doubts about my story as well. "She has arranged an appointment with the school counselor for Monday, Julia. As I've said to you before, you really need to speak to someone and she is qualified to deal with situations like this. Hopefully she can give you girls the help and advice you need to finally get over the issues you're having with each other."

My heart sank. She really was going to make me go back to school. And it looked like Sara was going to get away with what she had done. How on earth was I going to be able to face her on Monday? I sat up on my bed, propped up by pillows and watched my mother silently leave my room.

"I can't let her get away with this, I thought. "I just can't! But what am I going to do?"

My head spun with visions of Sara's gloating expression as I walked into the classroom on Monday morning. How on earth was I going to find the courage to face her? I prayed for a miracle but deep down I knew that she had outsmarted me again.

A cry for help…

As I sat in the school counselor's office on Monday morning, I was grateful at least for the chance to avoid class. I hadn't even seen Sara yet and was hoping that maybe she was having the day off school. It had been such a huge challenge to walk into the classroom as I was absolutely dreading the thought of coming face to face with her. But it did make me feel better when Millie and all the girls from my cabin surrounded me, asking about my hand and hoping that I was ok.

They'd all been led to believe that I had probably tripped on my way back from the bathroom and then landed on the broken glass that had mysteriously appeared outside our cabin. I decided that it was best to keep the truth to myself for the moment, for fear of making matters worse. But as I faced the counselor, sitting in a chair opposite me, I wondered how she would react to my story.

Throughout the course of the weekend, I'd had plenty of time to think and had come to the conclusion that I should take my mother's advice and tell the counselor everything. I was focusing on finally getting some help so that I could deal with Sara once and for all.

Last night, I had also decided to do some research on the internet and see what I could find out about bullying and how to cope with it. The one thing that clearly stood out was that if a person finds themselves in a situation where they are being bullied, they need to find someone to talk to for advice and help. I was surprised to find out that most people who are bullied, tend to keep the problem to themselves just like I've been doing. But this never solves anything. In fact, it usually makes matters worse. It's horrible not having anyone to confide in.

Miss Jennings, the counselor had a very kind and reassuring manner and I found her really easy to talk to. She sat and listened while I poured out the details and she didn't comment at all except for saying, "Go on, Julia, I'm listening," in a really encouraging and non-judgmental tone.

And the best part was that she actually seemed to believe my version of what had been going on.

She asked me how I reacted when I felt intimidated by Sara and I explained that she made me feel nervous and scared. Miss Jennings told me that this was where my problem was. She said that bullies often pick on people who have a weakness or who they can get a reaction from and if the bully is able to feel power, then they simply continue. She said that the secret to dealing with people like Sara is to hide your fear.

"You need to be confident around her, Julia. If she believes that she's not affecting you, she'll eventually get bored and stop."

"But it's not that easy!" I exclaimed. "Look at the things she's capable of. She's crazy and she's completely obsessed with upsetting me!"

"That's because she knows she can upset you," said Miss Jennings quietly. "The trick is to be confident and show her that you aren't upset anymore!"

"What are you good at, Julia? What do you like doing?" Miss Jennings asked.

"I love dancing," was my quick reply. "And a group of girls and I are entering the dance off competition in a couple of weeks. We're really hoping to win!"

"How do you feel, when you're dancing?" she continued. "Does it make you feel good inside?"

"Absolutely!" I replied. "I feel great when I'm dancing."

"Then that's it!" she said excitedly. "That's the feeling that you need to have, not just when you're dancing but all the time, and especially when you're around Sara. Show her that you are a confident person. Look her in the eye rather than looking away when she stares in your direction. And don't back down if she confronts you."

"I'm sure that isn't as easy as it sounds," I said to her. "No, it's not," was her reply. "But if you need to, then just fake it! Pretend that you're really confident even if you don't feel it. As long as she thinks that you are, then that's all that matters. And soon, it will come naturally to you and you won't have to fake it anymore."

"We can practice right here in my office," she suggested. "I'll pretend to be Sara giving you a hard time and you have a go at being the new confident Julia Jones."

"Okay," I hesitatingly agreed. "I'll give it a try."

At first it felt silly, standing tall with my shoulders back and looking Miss Jennings in the eye. I really struggled to look and sound confident, but after a while, it became easier and by the time I left her office, I almost felt like a different person.

Miss Jennings arranged for me to see her every day that week so I could practice acting and feeling sure of myself, rather than scared and fearful. And it just so happened that Sara wasn't at school after all. Apparently she was unwell, but I wondered if she was actually worrying about finally being caught out for what she had done to me at camp.

By the time she returned the following Monday, I was feeling pretty confident, I must admit. That was until I saw her face to face and then the familiar feelings of anxiety and fear started to take hold.

But Miss Jennings' words rushed through my mind. "Take a

deep breath, stand tall and look her in the eye. Remember, fake it if you have to!"

So that was what I did and the frown of confusion that crossed her face was enough to give me the courage to continue. "Hello Sara! Have you been too sick to come to school? Or has something else been worrying you? Do you know that you have an appointment with Miss Jennings today?"

I could barely believe that the confident voice I was hearing was actually coming from me. Then I strode straight past her, head up tall and shoulders back, smiling triumphantly at the glimpse of total shock that had appeared on her face. I flicked my hair to one side and kept walking.

I finally allowed myself to breathe. I was trembling slightly

at what I had just done and was worried that she might even come after me. But there had been no need. I had actually put her in her place for once and it felt so good!

The dance competition...

Finally the day of the dance competition arrived. The girls and I had been practicing every spare moment we had and felt that we were definitely ready. There were ten dance groups in all and I knew that we had some tough competition, particularly from Sara's group and also Blake's, but I felt confident that we'd at least make the top three.

The whole school was assembled in the hall ready for the concert to begin. I glanced across at Sara who was sitting nearby. She gave me a quick look and then turned towards the stage. Since my visits with Miss Jennings, the fear I used to feel whenever I was anywhere near Sara, had disappeared. I was now able to look her in the eye without feeling nervous or intimidated.

At first, she kept trying to embarrass or humiliate me at any opportunity, but I just knew that I had to stay strong. I began by pretending to feel totally confident even though I was shaking inside. Sometimes I even laughed at her nasty comments, making out they didn't bother me in the slightest. Then it didn't take long at all before I noticed that she was losing interest. She'd lost her power over me.

There was no scared reaction from me anymore so I guess there was no point in trying to antagonize me further. I could even see her friends were beginning to respect me. As I could no longer be pushed around, she stopped trying. And all it had taken was to develop some confidence.

I don't think I could have done it without my dancing though. Being involved in something that I'm good at has made me feel so much better about myself and given me the confidence boost that I desperately needed.

Waiting for our turn to perform, I thought back over the last few months and the nightmare I had experienced. It all seemed like a dream now and it was hard to believe that it had actually happened.

As I sat there, I wondered if Sara would look for someone else to bully. For some strange reason, people like her need to feel power over others as it helps them to feel good about themselves.

But as we were called on stage for our turn, all thoughts of Sara completely left my mind. I strode past her without a second glance, nervous but also excited to be performing in front of the whole school. As the music started, I spotted Blake Jansen looking towards me. Then to my huge surprise he nodded his head in encouragement and flashed me a winning smile.

It was such an amazing sensation to be on that stage doing something we loved and I knew afterwards that we had managed to blitz our dance. We all felt so proud! The applause was deafening!

Being handed the winner's trophy and a $200 voucher to share with my dance group was the biggest thrill I have ever had. And to top it all off, Blake was one of the first to congratulate us.

"You guys definitely deserved to win," he said sincerely.

Then, with a shy but hopeful look he asked, "Do you want to hang out together sometime, Julia? Maybe even during the holiday break?"

"Yeah, that'd be fun!" I replied, smiling happily.

And as we headed out of the hall together, I could see Sara's eyes following us. Not that I cared whatsoever. School was

over for the semester and I had a funny feeling that the
holidays were going to be better than ever!

What lies ahead for Julia Jones?
Has she overcome Sara's bullying once and for all?

And will Julia and Blake continue to be friends?

Find out in Book 3

Julia Jones' Diary – My Secret Dream

Read what others are saying about Julia Jones' Diary - Book 3...

-   *I think this book is really good and inspiring. If you want to know how to make your dreams come true, then read this book.*
-   *Great book! I mean I love all of your books they are inspiring. So I just want to say please don't stop writing ever!!*

Thank you
for reading my
book. If you liked
it could you please
leave a review?
Katrina

***

Please Like our Facebook page

to keep updated on the release date for each new book in the series...

www.facebook.com/JuliaJonesDiary

and follow us on Instagram:

@juliajonesdiary

Announcing a New Series!

Find out what lies ahead for Julia and all her friends in a brand new series...

<u>Mind Reader – Book 1: My New Life</u>

OUT NOW!!

This book introduces Emmie, a girl who unexpectedly arrives in Carindale and meets Millie. But Emmie has a secret, a secret that must remain hidden at all costs.
What happens to Julia, Blake, Sara and all the others and how does Emmie's sudden appearance impact Julia and her friends?
This fabulous new series continues the story of Julia Jones but has a whole new twist, one that all Julia Jones' Diary fans are sure to enjoy.

Announcing a New Series!

Exciting News! Katrina Kahler has continued to tell the story of Julia Jones - 3 years on - yes, the Teenage Years. Julia is older, but is she wiser? Whatever happened to Blake and Sara?

Grab the first new book in the series now! You'll love it!

Julia Jones – The Teenage years

Book 1: 'Falling Apart'

Out NOW!

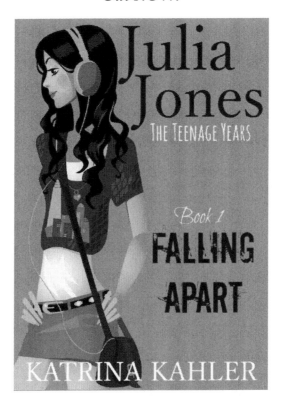

Here are some more books that you're sure to love!

***

Follow Julia Jones on Instagram @juliajonesdiary

And be sure to visit...

http://diaryofanalmostcoolgirl.com/

This is where you'll find all the bestselling books for kids!

Printed in Great Britain
by Amazon